Mouse and the BULLIES

Part 1

written by Jenny Alexander
illustrated by Jan Smith

Chapter One

Ha, Ha!

Mouse was surprised that Tom and Danny wanted to be friends with him. Years ago, they had teased him about his haircut, and he had got them into trouble over it. Jojo had told their mum, their mum had told Mr Hopkins, Mr Hopkins had told Mrs Turner and Mrs Turner had made Tom and Danny say sorry. They had more or less ignored him ever since.

But lately, Tom and Danny had started hanging round with him. Mouse was glad to have their company because most of his friends were busy doing other things at playtimes, and he was often bored. Jojo and Ravi always seemed to be at football practice, Ben and Donut were working on the school newsletter, Sam and Billy went to all the lunchtime clubs.

Tom and Danny said they liked Mouse because he was a good laugh, and they certainly did laugh a lot when the three of them were together. Whenever Mouse went up to them, Danny would say, in a fake Scottish accent, "There's a moose loose aboot this hoose!" and they would all collapse laughing.

"Ha, ha!" they laughed.

Whenever Mouse said anything, Tom would cup his hand behind his ear and say, "Did you squeak? I mean, did you speak?" Danny would put little pieces of cheese on Mouse's desk, and make nibbling noises.

"Ha, ha!" they laughed.

One day, when the three boys were putting the PE equipment away, Danny asked Tom, "Do you know how to turn a PE cupboard into a mousetrap?"

Tom said, "No."

Mouse went on stacking the mats.

"Like this!" said Danny, slamming the door, so that Mouse was trapped inside. He turned the key.

"Ha, ha, ha, ha, ha!" they laughed.

Mouse's name wasn't the only thing they found funny about him. They thought his clothes were hilarious. They called his favourite trainers, 'strainers,' because there was a small hole in one of them. They said his trousers were so baggy he must have borrowed them from his dad. They called his coat 'the banana skin,' just because it was yellow.

"Don't drop it on the floor," they would say. "Someone might slip over on it."

Tom and Danny particularly enjoyed talking about the old days.

"Do you remember that stupid haircut Mouse had?" Tom said.

"Ha, ha!" they laughed.

"And those letters old Turner made us write to him?" Danny said. "Ha, ha!"

"She thought we were really sorry!" Tom said.

"Ha, ha, ha, ha, ha!"

Chapter Two

A Horrible Thought

Not everyone was keen on Mouse being friends with Tom and Danny. Mrs Duffy said his behaviour in class had got much worse since he started to sit with them. She split them up, but then they just threw paper aeroplanes at each other across the room.

She was worried about Mouse's schoolwork, too. But Mouse didn't care. Tom and Danny said schoolwork was for girls. Not bothering with it was a great relief for Mouse, as it had always been a struggle for him.

Mouse's old friends didn't like Tom and Danny either, because they teased the younger ones in the playground. Tom and Danny couldn't see the problem. They were just having a laugh, they said.

"We're just having a laugh," said Mouse.

But Mouse tried not to think about what his old friends thought. They didn't understand. Tom and Danny called them the Goody-Goody Gang, and said they wouldn't know a good laugh if it came up and bit them on the nose.

Tom and Danny knew lots of other things besides how to have a good laugh. They knew how to look and how to act. They knew, for instance, that you couldn't have Space Superheroes on your schoolbag, like Mouse did.

"Only Reception kids have Space Superheroes on their schoolbags!" they exclaimed.

He couldn't believe that he had actually chosen that bag himself. He had liked it! Now he hated it. He was embarrassed by it. He would have to get a new one.

Mouse told his mum that he wanted a new schoolbag.

"But you haven't had the old one very long," she protested.

"The old one's stupid," said Mouse. "It's got Space Superheroes on it."

His mum was not impressed. "You can't have a new bag just because you've gone off the old one. We aren't made of money," she told him.

His mum didn't understand. Old people didn't understand anything, that's what Danny and Tom said. The point was, Mouse had to have a new schoolbag.

"I haven't just gone off it," he said. "It's broken. That's why I need a new one."

Mouse's mum looked at him, mistrustfully. She told him to go and fetch the bag. He ran up the stairs and went into his room. He grabbed it, tipped everything out, took a firm hold on either side of the zip and pulled as hard as he could. The end of the zip split open, and the fabric tore.

He took it downstairs to his mum.

"How did this happen?" she asked.

"It got caught on the coat hooks at school."

His mum sighed, and handed it back. Mouse knew that he had won.

But choosing a new schoolbag was easier said than done.

As soon as Mouse got to the High Street with his dad, he realised he still didn't know what sort to buy. He couldn't get one exactly the same as Tom's or Danny's, because that would look like copying. But he wasn't sure which other ones would make him look silly.

Mouse decided the best thing would be to choose a really expensive bag, because nobody laughed at money. But his dad did not agree. He couldn't see the point in spending a fortune when you could get a perfectly good schoolbag for much less, especially when Mouse's last one had got ruined so quickly. Mouse said that proved his point – if they had bought an expensive bag in the first place, it wouldn't have got broken.

He and his father argued about it in every shop, and it was the most miserable shopping trip they had ever had. In the end, they compromised, and both of them came home feeling grumpy. Mouse wished he could have had a more expensive bag, and his dad wished he had got a cheaper one.

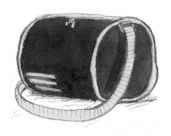

First, Mouse chose an expensive bag.

But his dad did not agree.

Then, he and his father argued.

In the end, both of them came home feeling grumpy.

Mouse couldn't see anything actually wrong with his new
schoolbag though, so he felt fairly confident Tom and Danny
wouldn't laugh at it. But when he got to school, Tom said,
sarcastically, "Nice bag! Did Minnie help you choose it?"
They called Jojo Minnie, as in Minnie Mouse. "Only it looks
like the sort of thing a girl would choose, doesn't it?"

"Being pink, and that," added Danny.

The bag was dark red. It was a colour Mouse had always
liked. Now, he hated it, and he hated himself for liking it.
He felt like crying over his own stupidity.

"Eek! Is that the time?" Danny exclaimed, looking at
his watch.

"Eek, eek!" squeaked Tom.

"Ha, ha!" they both laughed.

They raced off to the classroom, leaving Mouse alone, trying to laugh. It wasn't easy, when the joke was on you. Suddenly, it occurred to Mouse that the joke was usually on him. In fact, it was always on him.

Then Mouse had a horrible thought. What if Tom and Danny didn't really like him? What if they only wanted someone to make fun of? Could it be that Tom and Danny weren't really his friends at all?

Chapter Three

Leave Me Alone!

Mouse tried to avoid Tom and Danny at playtime. He needed time to think. But they kept finding him. They made lots of mouse jokes. Mouse couldn't bring himself to laugh. Danny said, "What's wrong, Mouse? Cat got your tongue?"

"Ha, ha!" they both laughed.

At dinner time, they came looking for him again, because
Danny had a new idea. There was another kind of mouse –
a computer mouse. You pushed it around a mat. He grabbed
Mouse by the shoulders and steered him round. Tom took over.
They laughed and laughed, "Ha, ha!"

"Leave me alone!" they mimicked him, in high, squeaky voices. They scurried around him, with their hands curled in front of their faces, pretending to be mice. "Ha, ha, ha, ha, ha!" they both sniggered.

Mouse still wasn't laughing. They stopped.
   "He doesn't want to play with us any more," said Danny.
   "But he hasn't got much choice ..."
   "Because we want to play with him."

18

Mouse remembered once seeing Fatcat with a mouse. She threw it up in the air, jumped on it and pushed it from one paw to the other. The mouse was injured and frozen with fear. Fatcat was only playing – but it was a deadly game for the mouse.

After that, however hard Mouse tried to shake Tom and Danny off, he couldn't. They followed him everywhere. They never stopped picking on him. It got so bad that Mouse dreaded going to school.

His home life suffered too. He blamed his mum and dad for what was happening to him. It was their fault he had stupid clothes and a stupid name. He was angry with Jojo, because no one ever teased her, and it wasn't fair. But most of all, he was angry with Pip, because he could still play with Space Superheroes and he didn't care about his name.

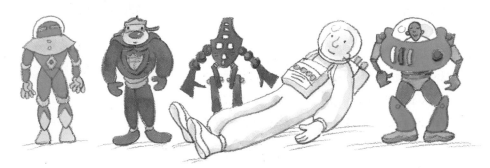

Mouse started to pick on Pip. One day, when their mother was peeling cooking apples at the sink, Mouse said to his brother, "Do you want an apple, Pip?"

Pip flew his last Space Superhero safely onto the Starship Waste Bin and looked up. "Yes, please," he said. Mouse took an apple pip from the chopping board and offered it to him. Pip frowned.

"Get it?" said Mouse. "An apple, Pip. An apple pip!" Mouse laughed, but Pip was angry. He stood up and tugged at their mother's sleeve. "I want an apple!" he said.

"You can't have one. They aren't cooked yet," she replied.

"I want one. Mouse said I could."

He stamped his foot.

Their mother sighed, and gave him a piece of apple. "You won't like it," she warned. "It's a cooking apple. It'll be sour."

Pip, looking pleased with himself, put the apple in his mouth. He chewed briefly, screwed up his face, and then spat it out in a stream of dribble. It landed – splat! – on Space Superhero Steve, and knocked him off the rubbish bin. Pip began to wail. Mouse laughed and laughed.

Another time, when the family was sitting round the table having tea, Mouse said, "Look! There's an orange pip."

"Where?" they all asked.

He tipped his glass over, and orange juice poured down into Pip's lap. "There!" said Mouse, pointing at Pip.

Nobody was laughing.

"Why did you do that?" Mr Macdonald said.

"It was a joke," said Mouse.

"It was a horrible thing to do."

Mrs Macdonald sent Pip to find some dry trousers. She looked at Mouse. "Why are you being so mean?" she said.

"You've been like a bear with a sore head for weeks," added Mr Macdonald. "What on earth is the matter with you, Mouse?"

Mouse pushed back his chair and stood up. He thought they were all getting at him. "Leave me alone!" he yelled.

He ran upstairs and shut himself in his room. He flung himself down on the bed.

In the cage beside him, Ricky was jumping about. He climbed up the bars and pushed his nose through. All his wonderful whiskers were twitching with excitement, he was so happy to see Mouse.

Mouse leaned over and opened the cage door. Ricky dropped down onto the desk, and then onto the bed. He ran up and down, jumping over the big folds of the duvet. When he had worked off some of his energy, he ran onto Mouse's chest. He put his paws on Mouse's chin and licked his lips.

Everyone else found it revolting when Ricky did that. But it tickled so much, it always made Mouse laugh. Then Ricky would get a chance to lick his teeth, and everyone would cry out in disgust.

Mouse wasn't feeling ticklish. Ricky stopped licking him and sat back on his hind legs. He seemed to sense something was wrong. Mouse sighed. "Everything's a mess, Ricky," he said. "I just don't know what to do."

Chapter Four

Desperate Measures

Mouse knew he couldn't go on forever being picked on by Danny and Tom. It was tearing his whole life apart. He was tempted to tell on them. That had worked last time, with the haircut business. But they were bigger now. If he told, and things got worse, they might beat him up or something. He was bigger now, too. He ought to be able to sort his problems out for himself.

In the school library, there were some books about bullying. No one ever took them out, because then everyone would know that he or she had a problem. But Mouse was desperate. He slipped one under his jumper and took it home, without getting it checked out.

The book had lots of advice. Some of it didn't sound too good to Mouse, but he decided to try it anyway. What had he got to lose? Besides, it was in a book, so it was bound to work.

Practise walking with your back straight and your shoulders back. You'll feel bigger and more confident and people will be less likely to pick on you.

Mouse practised walking tall in his bedroom until his mum came up and stopped him. She said he would wear a hole in the carpet. Then he practised in the park, when no one else was around. It really did make him feel better.

At last, he was ready to try it at school. He sauntered across the road and strode through the school gates. Danny and Tom were waiting for him. "Look at Mouse! He looks like a robot!" they said.

Everyone looked round. Mouse crumpled. His confidence streamed out of him. He had never felt so little in his life.

But he did not give up. He looked for something else to try.

Most of Danny and Tom's jokes were about Mouse's nickname. Mouse thought long and hard about how he might answer them back. Eventually, he had it! He waited for Danny to say, "There's a moose loose aboot this hoose," and then ... Mouse's mind went blank. He couldn't remember what he had planned to say. But he had to say something. "Get lost!" he cried.

Danny and Tom exchanged a look. They raised their eyebrows. They said, "Oooh!"

"Get lost!" mimicked Danny, in a high wavering voice.

"Get lost!" echoed Tom.

Mouse went back to his book.

He couldn't do that. They would never believe him. He would never believe himself! He was a complete failure. He slipped the book back onto the library shelf, feeling more hopeless and helpless than ever.

But as he left school, he noticed the ChildLine card pinned up on a notice board. It had been there for so long that the writing had almost faded clean away. The phone number was very easy to remember: 0800 1111.

He could still remember the number when he got home.
He remembered it all through tea, and when everyone had
settled down to watch their favourite programme, he still had
not forgotten it.

All alone in the hall, Mouse dialled the number. He heard
the ringing tone, and then a woman's voice.

"Hello. You're through to ChildLine ..."

The woman said her name was Judy. She told Mouse he didn't have to give his name if he didn't want to, and everything he said would be confidential – she wouldn't tell anyone. She wouldn't try to interfere in any way. She was just there for someone to talk to. But Mouse couldn't talk. He felt as if he had a heavy stone in his throat.

Judy asked Mouse if someone was being nasty to him. Suddenly, all the anger Mouse had stored up inside him melted away, and a wave of grief swept over him. He began to cry. Judy kept talking to him. She told him he had done well to have the courage to phone. She understood how hard that had been.

Mouse just stood there, crying into the phone. He thought she would hang up, but she didn't. She tried to reassure him. Eventually, he wiped his face on his sleeve and sniffed back the last of his tears. The heavy stone had gone. He was able to tell her about the teasing. She asked him, "What sort of things do they say?" and "How does it feel when they talk to you like that?"

Judy asked Mouse how long the teasing had been going on. Was anyone else being teased? Had Mouse told anyone about it? Was there someone at home he could talk to? Was there someone at school?

Mouse told Judy there was no one he could talk to. He didn't want to talk. He just wanted to make Tom and Danny stop teasing him. But before she could tell him how to do this, Mouse heard a noise behind him. He turned round. Jojo was standing in the living room doorway.

Mouse put down the phone.

Chapter Five

Jojo Messes Things Up

"How long have you been there?" asked Mouse.

"Long enough," said his sister.

"What are you going to do?"

"Tell Mum, of course. Like you should've done."

Mouse frowned. If his mum found out, she would go straight down to school. He didn't want everyone to know that Tom and Danny had been teasing him, and that he couldn't handle it on his own.

"Don't do that," he said. "It's my problem, and I want to sort it out my own way."

The television went off, and the living room door swung open. Their dad came out, carrying Pip on his back. He took Pip upstairs for a bath. Their mum came out, looking for the television magazine. She stopped when she saw them.

"What's going on?" she asked.

"Nothing," said Mouse.

"Jojo?"

"Nothing's going on," said Jojo.

Their mother shrugged and went into the kitchen. Mouse thanked his sister for not telling.

"I'll give you a week," she said. "But if you haven't sorted it out by then, we're doing it my way."

Mouse thought his sister was being unfair. By sorting it out, she just meant telling someone. But he wasn't going to tell on Danny and Tom. There had to be another way.

However, over the next few days, while Mouse was trying to work out a way of dealing with Danny and Tom, things went from bad to worse. The fact that Jojo knew, and was watching him all the time, added to his embarrassment and shame.

Tom and Danny had been careful not to let anyone see what they were doing. There were no notes this time – no evidence. They had got older and sneakier since the haircut thing. Nobody had noticed how it was between them and Mouse this time.

Now, Jojo saw when they 'accidentally' jogged Mouse, or knocked his pens on the floor, or shut the door in his face. She heard the 'jokes' that made them snigger in class, and laugh out loud in the playground. Mouse couldn't bear the humiliation.

Even worse, Mouse was terrified Jojo would tell the others. She had promised not to tell their parents or teachers, but she might tell their friends. Then everyone would see what was going on, and know how pathetic he was.

Mouse was so worried that he couldn't concentrate in class. It didn't help that Danny kept poking him in the ribs with a ruler. He hardly heard a thing Mrs Duffy said. He only realised she had asked a question when a forest of hands sprang up.

"Mouse Macdonald!" said Mrs Duffy, ignoring the hands. "Would you like to tell us the answer?"

Unable to think of a good lie, Mouse had no choice but to tell her the truth. "I wasn't listening, Mrs Duffy."

Everyone in the class was listening now. The teacher frowned. "Of course you weren't listening," she cried. "You were too busy messing about with Tom and Danny. I've had just about enough of you three never paying attention!"

41

Mouse sat staring at the table. Out of the corner of his eye, he saw Jojo put her hand up.

"What is it, Jojo?" snapped the teacher.

"Please, Mrs Duffy – it's not my brother's fault. Danny was digging him in the ribs with a ruler. He and Tom are always picking on Mouse."

Mouse flashed an angry look at his sister. She thought she had sorted things out for him, but he was sure she had just messed things up.

Chapter Six

In Deep Water

Mrs Duffy sighed and closed her book. She put it down on her desk. "I can understand you wanting to stick up for your brother," she told Jojo. "But Mouse has been just as noisy and disruptive as the others since he moved onto that table."

Jojo opened her mouth to say something, but Mrs Duffy stopped her. "That's enough!" she said. "Mouse, Tom and Danny, come out here. The rest of you, do the next exercise."

Thirty faces were bent over their books, but sixty eyes were on the drama being played out at the front of the classroom. They heard Mrs Duffy ask the three boys if they had anything to say for themselves. None of them spoke up. Mouse nearly did. He was already in deep water, and things couldn't get much worse. But he hesitated, and the chance was lost.

Mrs Duffy gave them a serious telling-off. One by one, she made them squirm. When it was Mouse's turn, the other two grinned at each other, secretly. Mrs Duffy saw it, and she was furious. She turned on them.

"So, you find this funny, do you?" she said, sharply. "Well, if I have any more trouble from you two, you will be going to see Mrs Turner. Let's see how funny you find that!"

Mrs Duffy put the three boys on different tables. While they were collecting their things, she asked the others, "Who has finished the next exercise?" All the hands stayed down.
Mrs Duffy was not very pleased.

In his new place, Mouse glanced at the clock. Twenty minutes until home-time. Twenty minutes – and then his life would not be worth living. But after school, Ben and Donut went over to Mouse's table to talk to him. Ravi joined them. They all went together to get their coats and bags.

Jojo and Sam were waiting for them in the playground. Now that they knew what the problem was, his friends all wanted to protect him. They didn't give Tom and Danny a chance to get Mouse on his own.

But the next day, when Jojo and Ravi were at football practice, Sam and Billy were at chess club, and Ben and Donut were working on the newsletter, Tom and Danny came looking for Mouse.

"There's a moose loose ..." They looked as friendly as could be. Mouse felt nervous.

"You know, someone ought to tell that Minnie Mouse sister of yours that you shouldn't tell on people," said Danny.

"You could get them into trouble," added Tom.

He pretended to be Mrs Duffy. "If there's any more trouble from you two, you will be going to see Mrs Turner."

"Ha, ha!" they laughed.

"But there won't be any more trouble, will there, Mouse?" said Danny. "Because you're going to make sure Minnie stops sticking her nose in. Right?"

He put his fist on Mouse's upper arm, and gave him
a gentle shove. "See, if there's any more trouble from you,
you will be talking to ... my brother," he growled.

Mouse remembered Danny's brother. He had been the
school bully when Mouse and his friends were in the infants.
Mouse had managed to steer clear of him – but he had seen
what happened to people who didn't.

Tom said, "Danny's brother is very good at pest control."

"And do you know what sort of pests he really hates?"
said Danny. "Mice!"

"Ha, ha, ha, ha, ha!" they laughed.

How does Mouse deal with the bullies?
Find out in Mouse and the Bullies Part 2.